At that very moment, Kiviat's heavily armed expedition was chugging up the river, entering Kaleri country.

That evening, George built a blind of branches to conceal himself and Susan. As he slept, Susan watched the dinosaurs throughout the night. When George awoke, he found her peering through binoculars at the brontosaurus family. Many pages of notes were at her feet.

"They sleep in the water," she informed him excitedly. "Their bodies are so heavy, they stay partially submerged. The female cuddled the baby." Susan kissed him. "I'm glad you built this thing."

George nodded. "As long as they can't see us, we're safe," he said.

A loud "Har-rew!" sounded behind them. George and Susan whirled. Papa dinosaur towered above them, lordly and indifferent to their presence. As he lumbered off calmly, Susan giggled. Sheepishly, George said, "Well, I guess we can get a little closer to them."

Later that day, George climbed a tree to pick molombos. After gathering an armful of the fruit, he and Susan cautiously approached the three dinosaurs and placed the food on the ground as an offering.

As Mama brontosaurus lumbered forward and sniffed the molombos, Susan said, "If we can get them used to us, maybe we can attach one of Kenge's radio chips on them. That would stake our claim."

A few hours later, as Mama and Papa dinosaur ate in the clearing, George and Susan swam in the lake. As they splashed happily, Baby watched them. Seeing their clothes piled on the bank, the little dinosaur swam over and sniffed around. Susan's eyeglasses were on top of the pile. Boldly, Baby dug her nose into the stack and burrowed, honking.

The next thing George and Susan saw was Baby swimming alongside with Susan's glasses stuck comically on her nose! The tiny brontosaurus blinked. Susan squinted.

"Get the transmitter," said George. "Maybe we can attach it now."

"It's as good a time as any," answered Susan, climbing out of the water and tossing the chip to George. "Be careful," she warned.

George edged toward Baby who eyed him suspiciously. They circled each other, treading water. Baby honked warily. George tried to sneak up behind the little dinosaur, but Baby ducked underwater. George ducked under, too, but then Baby came up. When George came up, Baby went down. Like jack-in-the-boxes, George and Baby popped up and down until George, exasperated, lunged at the infant brontosaurus with a mighty splash. But Baby slipped away with ease.

Watching from the shore, Susan laughed. Then George decided to try a submarine approach. Diving, he swam under the murky water. Unable to see his prey, he bobbed up, gulped air, and dove again. Suddenly, he was face to face with Baby who had her mouth open and teeth bared. It was a shock for both of them! They fled in opposite directions, Baby swimming for shore, and George paddling toward the center of the lake.

Standing on the bank, Susan tempted the tiny brontosaurus with some fruit. "There, there, Baby, it's all right," she said. "George, you scared her."

Baby climbed out of the water as Susan continued to gesture with the

fruit. "Here, sweetheart," she cooed invitingly. "Free meal."

Then, a surprising thing happened. The baby dinosaur waddled over, took the fruit out of Susan's hand, and began to eat it!

Susan smiled, marveling, "I don't believe it." Baby rubbed against Susan playfully. Susan laughed, and Baby rolled over like a puppy. Susan scratched Baby's stomach and caused her to honk with delight. Amazed, Susan exclaimed, "She's playing! Dinosaurs don't play."

"You're too scientific," said George. Climbing out of the water, he quickly snapped the transmitter band onto one of Baby's upraised legs.

Mama dinosaur screamed from across the clearing, "Har-rew! Har-rew!" As George and Susan crouched and peered through the trees, they saw Kiviat leading his expedition in a wild attempt to capture Mom.

It was Nigel who stepped forward with a tranquilizer gun and shot a dart into Mama brontosaurus's neck. Kiviat shouted, "Again!" and Nigel fired once more. Mama howled, then, confused and drugged, stumbled backward. Kiviat's men quickly threw a rope around her, pulled, and the huge dinosaur sank to her knees.

George and Susan watched from their vantage point among the trees. Baby shivered behind them.

Enraged, Papa dinosaur now charged from the jungle to defend his mate. The gigantic brontosaurus snarled viciously and raised his massive foot to attack the villains. Panicking, the soldiers ran. Other soldiers, however, unseen by Kiviat, raised their machine guns and fired. The bullets hit their mark. His mate cried out, terrified. Papa staggered toward her, as if for a last goodbye, but he couldn't make it. With his strength gone, he reeled backward and fell, splashing into the lake...dead.

Kiviat angrily confronted Colonel Nsogbu. "That was a one-of-a-kind specimen!"

"No," countered Nsogbu, pointing toward Mom. "*That* is a one-of-a-kind specimen."

Shocked and horrified, George instructed Susan to hide Baby, then stepped forth from the bush. He grabbed Kiviat from behind. "Some scientist!" he cried angrily. "Were you going to have them stuffed?"

Colonel Nsogbu demanded, "Professor, who is this?"

Kiviat removed George's hand and said, "Mr. Loomis, kindly *shut up*!" Turning to the soldiers, Kiviat directed, "Get a rope on that back leg. Secure it."

George shouted, "No! You're letting her go!" Shoving the soldiers out of his way, George began untying the ropes. In an instant, Colonel Nsogbu signaled to a soldier. A rifle butt hit George on the head. Moaning, George slumped to the ground.

In the trees, holding Baby, who was frightened and confused, Susan stifled a scream.

Pointing his gun at George, the soldier asked Kiviat, "Is he your prisoner?"

Kiviat shrugged and said, "We don't take prisoners."

As the soldier stiffened and tightened his finger on the trigger, Susan burst from the trees. "DON'T! YOU FIEND! DON'T!" she cried.

The soldier whirled and pointed his gun at Susan. George, coming to, shouted, "Susan, get back!" The soldier was about to fire when suddenly he reeled backward and collapsed, a blowgun dart protruding from his neck.

Cephu, the Kaleri chief, shouted a defiant war cry from the jungle. Darts and arrows filled the air. Terrified, Sergeant Gambwe shouted, "Kaleri! Take cover!" The soldiers hit the ground and fired their machine guns into the jungle, but the tribesmen were gone.

George scrambled to his feet and shouted, "Run, Susan! Run!" Together, they fled for the trees. Instantly, the soldiers fired at them.

Baby, cowering just a few yards away, honked in terror and scurried into the forest.

With bullets dancing at their feet, George and Susan leaped into the trees. Three soldiers started to follow them, but Colonel Nsogbu ordered them to stop. "They aren't worth the effort." Turning to Kiviat, Nsogbu asked, "Do you still want to set up your lab in Kaleri country, professor?"

Considering the situation, Kiviat stared at Mama brontosaurus, who was moaning pitifully. Grimacing, he said, "We'll have to take the dinosaur back."

Baby wandered alone through the jungle. The sun was setting and she had never been without her parents before. Reaching a tiny cove, she slowly turned circles. Then, whimpering softly, she lay down. Tears formed in her sad eyes. She was confused and lonely, as never before.

It was heartbreaking, the worst night of the little dinosaur's life.

In the morning, Baby woke up and yawned, squeaking. Instinctively, she headed back to the lake. She found her father, dead, his head out of the water with a buzzard perched on his neck. The bird hissed at Baby, but she raised her foot threateningly, and the creature flew off. Stepping forward, Baby sniffed her father, then nudged him with her nose, but he didn't move.

Not understanding why, Baby honked pitifully.

Also returning to the lake, George and Susan made their way stealthily out of the trees. Their field camp has been ransacked. Hearing Baby's mournful honks, they approached the little dinosaur, feeling sorry for her. When Baby saw them, however, she jumped back, frightened, distrusting humans. George coaxed, "Come on, pal. We're friends, remember?"

Susan added, "It's okay, Baby..."

Baby whipped her tail around to protect herself, then ran off into the rain forest. George and Susan went after her, but she was already gone.

Susan said, "George, if we caught her, maybe we could beat Eric back. It would be *our* discovery."

Baby sniffed through some trash left by Kiviat's expedition. Looking for something to eat, she stuck her head into an old, ripped duffel bag, but no sooner had she done so than she realized she was trapped. Honking, Baby thrashed wildly. Snagging the bag on a branch, she pulled free, but there, resting on her head like a turban, was a pair of shorts. Squeaking, Baby shook her neck, and the underwear floated to the ground.

Then Baby heard a familiar sound, "Har-rew! Har-rew!" It was her mother's cry! Wiggling happily, Baby ran off toward the sound. But sadly, all the little dinosaur found was Susan's tape recorder playing Mom and Dad's cries at full volume.

Hiding just yards away in their tent, George and Susan watched. "This is almost cruel," said George.

"Shhhh," whispered Susan. "She'll see the fruit soon."

Baby sniffed the tape recorder cautiously, then nudged it. She heard her parents' voices, then her own. Whimpering, Baby picked up the recorder in her mouth. Then she saw the molombos, strategically piled outside the tent flap. Baby ambled over, sniffing the food hungrily.

In an instant, George leaped from the tent and flung Susan's web belt around Baby's neck. Yelping, Baby yanked and ran, dragging George through the camp. Susan scrambled out. At last George tackled Baby and held her down.

Frightened, Baby honked, looking up at her captors. Susan, testing Baby's friendliness, sat down alongside her. The little dinosaur cooed, cuddling. Charmed, George smiled as Susan rubbed Baby's stomach affectionately.

Meanwhile, Mama brontosaurus was being kidnapped by Kiviat. Tranquilized and lashed to a bamboo raft, she moaned pitifully as the Colonel's exhausted soldiers poled her down the narrow river. The ropes biting into her skin hurt terribly. In desperation, she jostled her body and waved her head. Her movements rocked the raft, making the expedition's progress even more difficult.

Sergeant Gambwe, directing the activity, cursed angrily at Mama dinosaur. When she didn't keep still, he used his rifle butt to beat her.

Enraged, Kiviat demanded, "Colonel. Stop that idiot!"

Colonel Nsogbu commanded, "Stop, Sergeant! Now!"

The sergeant obeyed reluctantly. At the colonel's order, a soldier aimed a tranquilizer gun at Mama. Kiviat protested, "No! She's had too much already!" But it was too late.

The dart hit Mama brontosaurus in the neck and almost instantly her head slumped into the water. Nigel rushed over, screaming, "She'll drown! A rope, quickly!" Nigel grabbed her massive head, but couldn't lift it. A soldier tossed him a rope and Nigel dove into the river. He looped the rope around Mom's head, and the men on deck pulled her out.

Hurriedly, Kiviat prepared an antidote. Dripping wet, Nigel injected Mom's neck. Slowly, she came to. Kiviat was furious. They had barely managed to save her life.

George, Susan and Baby followed a riverside path. Baby was very happy, and the three friends made good progress.

Soon, however, the path ended and they were forced to cut inland. Hiking through the thick jungle was much more difficult. Baby felt uncomfortable away from the water. Often, George had to hack away clusters of vines with a machete to clear a trail. After many hours, George collapsed and said, "I think one of my blisters just pulled a muscle."

Susan consoled him, describing the Nobel and Pulitzer prizes they would win if they could outrace Kiviat back to civilization. Behind them, Baby honked mournfully, trying to climb a molombo tree. At Susan's insistence George shinnied up the trunk for the fruit.

"If my figures are right," calculated Susan, "Baby eats about two hundred pounds a day."

Reaching for the fruit, George joked, "I wish I had two hundred arms."

That night, George and Susan were awakened by moanings from Baby, who poked her head through the tent flap. Susan asked, "What's wrong, Baby?" She offered the infant brontosaurus an apple. "Still hungry?" Seeing the food, Baby groaned even louder. "*Oh*," said Susan. "Well, you know, nobody told you to make such a pig of yourself!" Susan gave Baby a motherly pat. "You'll live."

Susan settled back into her sleeping bag. Suddenly, Baby emitted a deafening moan. Susan and George jumped. Baby had come into the tent and was standing over them! "You want to sleep in here?" asked Susan.

Honking, Baby plopped down, half in between and half on top of them.

"No," George whined. "Get her out."

Baby groaned pathetically and nuzzled against Susan who rubbed her belly and said, "She doesn't feel well. She's just a baby. It'll be all right."

Cooing, Baby stretched out for more room, pinning George and Susan against the tent.

As the stakes were pulled out, and the tent fell over, George moaned, "Good grief..."

The next morning, George, Susan and Baby continued on their trek. George led the way. At times he had to pull Susan and Baby over the rugged terrain.

Once, climbing a tree for Baby's molombos, George was attacked by wasps. Tired and angry, George rubbed mud on his painful bites. Slapping an ant on his leg, he wailed, "Even my bites have bites."

More concerned for Baby, Susan looked her over for stings. Then, businesslike, she said, "George, we're not far from the village."

"Susan," George whined, "these wasps have turned my arm into hamburger."

Surprised at his irritation, Susan said, "I'm sorry."

Baby waddled up and nuzzled between them, demanding affection from her "parents." George snapped, "Not now, Yo-Yo. Eat your molombos. They were hard enough to get."

Sharply, Susan said, "It's not her fault."

"I'm not blaming anybody. My arm hurts!"

Susan raised her voice, "Why are you yelling?"

George screamed, "I'M NOT YELLING!"

Upset at their arguing, Baby nuzzled Susan again, seeking motherly love. Distracted, Susan shoved the little dinosaur away. "In a minute, Baby!" she told her.

George and Susan's argument raged on. When Baby tried to interrupt once more, both of them pushed her away. As their yelling intensified, the poor infant brontosaurus turned, miserable and unnoticed, and slunk sadly off into the jungle.

As darkness covered the rain forest, Baby wandered through the eerie moonlight. Lost and frightened, she decided to return to George and Susan.

Vicious growling stopped her. A terrifying warthog stepped out of the

trees, his sharp tusks glinting. The snorting animal advanced.

Baby froze, then tried to honk. Nothing came forth but a tiny squeak. Terrified, Baby turned and ran. Without looking back, the infant dinosaur fled as fast as she could, deeper and deeper into the jungle. When she finally stopped, Baby had no idea which way to go. A chorus of animal calls surrounded her.

Whimpering, she curled up under a molombo tree, looking up hungrily at the fruit. Finally, frightened and lonely, she fell into a fitful, nightmarish sleep.

The next morning, Baby was awakened by an elephant's trumpeting call. Peeking out from behind a tree, Baby saw a large Mama elephant leading two calves through the forest. Baby imagined they looked very much like her. They had big rumps, blocky feet, and wrinkled skin. The trunks were somewhat peculiar, but she could overlook that, since they swayed like a dinosaur's neck.

Bouncing happily, Baby strolled out and joined the elephant family, bringing up the rear. Waddling next to the smallest calf, she honked, saying hello. The young elephant, nearly Baby's size, squeaked back happily. In no time at all, they were friends, honking and squeaking as they continued on their way.

Mama elephant, however, hearing an intruder, turned and trumpeted angrily at Baby. Surprised, Baby skittered back. When Baby tried again to follow the family, the big elephant blocked her way. Saddened, Baby stared up at the Mama elephant and honked questioningly. In reply, the elephant lowered her trunk and pushed the little dinosaur down a hill.

Baby rolled through the grass and landed in a thicket. Dazed, she watched the elephants disappear from view. Then she picked herself up, dejected, and wandered on alone.

Sick with worry, George and Susan tried to track Baby. Susan called out Baby's name as George tinkered with Kenge's radio, trying to pick up the beeping signal from the transmitter band on Baby's leg.

Meanwhile, Baby wandered through the jungle in the opposite direction, very tired and extremely hungry. Stumbling over a root, she fell and hit her head. Looking around, she saw some half-rotten molombos that had fallen to the ground. They were quickly gobbled up. With a daily two-hundred-pound appetite, Baby was nearly starving.

Suddenly, George picked up a signal. Quickly, Susan and he followed it, heading back toward the river. As the beeping grew louder, their hopes rose.

When they reached the river, however, they stopped to hide behind a

large tree. Across the water was Kiviat's camp, where a large camouflaged helicopter was landing in a cloud of dust. Soldiers jumped out of it, joining other armed men who were gathered around Baby's captive mother.

"I must have picked up a stray signal from Kiviat's traveling circus over there," explained George. "I don't see Baby anywhere."

At Colonel Nsogbu's direction, the soldiers tried to force the huge dinosaur to stand, prodding the poor creature with poles. Drugged and exhausted, Mom rose slightly, but then collapsed.

Tears welled in Susan's eyes. Weeping, she said, "George, we'll have to help her."

Later that day, Nigel examined Mama brontosaurus. Peering into her glazed eyes and touching her skin, he looked very displeased.

Leaving to discuss his sad findings with Kiviat, Nigel didn't notice George and Susan hanging onto a log that drifted across the river toward Mama dinosaur's raft. The guards assigned to the captive dinosaur were dozing.

George and Susan climbed out of the water, trying not to make a sound. The female brontosaurus stirred. Stroking her tenderly, Susan whispered, "Don't worry, Mom. We'll get you back to your Baby. Quiet now, shhhh."

Mom recognized her human friends as they untied her. She cried softly. Susan soothed her as George tugged at the ropes. Groaning, Mom put her nose against Susan. Then, suspiciously, the brontosaurus sniffed and growled.

Whispering, George said, “It's your belt. She smells Baby.”

Susan moved away, but it was too late. Upset and concerned, Mama dinosaur *har-rewed* angrily and strained with renewed strength at the remaining ropes.

It didn't take long before Mom's guards woke up and rushed toward George and Susan.

With a snap, Mom's tail broke free and whipped into the guards, flinging one like a rag doll against a tree. His rifle fired harmlessly.

The camp came to life. George and Susan dashed for the river. Spotting them, the soldiers fired warning shots above their heads. Wisely, then, George and Susan froze with their hands up.

Meanwhile, Mama dinosaur's temper tantrum intensified. Enraged, she twisted violently, breaking even more of her bonds, her tail smashing the raft. Terrified, the army men took aim with their machine guns. Kiviat rushed to Colonel Nsogbu and pleaded, "For God's sake, don't let them shoot!"

The Colonel barked an order, and the men held their fire. Sergeant Gambwe then stepped forward with a tranquilizer gun. The dart hit Mama brontosaurus's neck.

Howling with rage, the massive dinosaur wavered, then collapsed. Kiviat rushed to tend to her, passing Susan who chided, "Eric, how can you treat her like this?"

Attending the unconscious dinosaur, Kiviat turned to tell Gambwe, "Don't harm them.... Susan, I'll speak to you later."

Moments later, accused of trying to steal the dinosaur, George and Susan were led away and imprisoned as criminals of the state.

That night, two armed soldiers guarded George and Susan in a special tent. When Kiviat entered, slightly drunk, his eyes looked wild and crazy. Grinning weirdly at Susan, he said, "A brontosaurus hatchling, eh? An amazing find. I've read your notes - unschooled but impressive. Tell me about the radio transceiver."

Susan frowned. She now hated Kiviat. "I don't know of any hatchling," she said.

Kiviat snarled insanely. "You have no idea what this dinosaur means to me," he told her. "I've been ridiculed for years. 'Eric Kiviat's off chasing dinosaurs,' they said. All this time *I was right.* Nobody's going to steal the glory from me now! Everyone who ever laughed at this crazy professor will apologize the day I'm knighted. . . ."

Kiviat stopped suddenly, lost in some mad thought. Then his eyes darted between George and Susan. Growling, he insisted, "I shall find the hatchling...and *you* will help me."

Kiviat stormed out. Nigel intercepted him. Anguished, Nigel said, "Eric, the animal's heartbeat is irregular. Nsogbu plans to fly her back in the helicopter. She'll never survive it. What do we do?"

In a menacing voice, Kiviat muttered, "I'll deal with the colonel."

At midnight, Kiviat entered Colonel Nsogbu's tent. Smiling politely, Kiviat said, "Colonel, the dinosaur's restless. I've prepared a new serum." Kiviat showed Nsogbu a tranquilizer vial.

"Good," answered Nsogbu. He reached for his tranquilizer gun, opened the chamber, and gestured for Kiviat to hand him the vial.

Instead, Eric grinned and took the gun out of Nsogbu's hand. "*I'd* better. The bottle's a bit delicate," he explained.

Kiviat then aimed the gun toward Nsogbu and shot a poison dart right into his heart. The Colonel grabbed his chest and started to scream, but Kiviat fastened his hand over the dying man's mouth. A moment later, Nsogbu slumped to the ground. He was Kiviat's second murder victim.

The next morning, Sergeant Gambwe and his soldiers dragged George and Susan across the compound. Kiviat emerged from his tent and asked innocently, "What's going on?"

"They say we killed the colonel," exclaimed George.

Gambwe handed Kiviat the tranquilizer syringe. "We found this in their belongings," he said.

Kiviat examined the evidence he had planted and said, "Yes, it confirms my suspicions. They're working for the CIA."

"WHAT?" shouted Susan.

George yelled, "You're crazy, Kiviat. We're not—"

Gambwe smacked George across the face, then barked commands to his men, who shoved George and Susan against a tree. Wielding machine guns, the soldiers formed a firing squad.

Kiviat stepped forward, "Sergeant, don't! We need—"

"They die!" interrupted Gambwe.

"No," insisted Kiviat. "There's treasure. They buried American gold. With our radio receiver they can lead us to it."

Interested, Gambwe looked at George and Susan, then studied Kiviat.

An hour later, Mama dinosaur watched soldiers force George and Susan into the army helicopter. The brontosaurus seemed to recognize the machine, almost as if it were a prehistoric bird.

The helicopter took off. Kiviat, Gambwe and an armed guard sat behind George and Susan. Kiviat fiddled with a powerful radio receiver, tuning in to Baby's frequency. When the radio beeped loudly, Kiviat smiled. "Got it!"

George and Susan looked at each other grimly.

Below, in the jungle, Baby was playing happily with a new friend—a

mongoose. Bouncing joyously, Baby cornered the little creature. Squeaking, the mongoose darted for freedom. Baby jumped after it, but a strange noise distracted her. She looked up. Hovering above was the frightening helicopter.

Kiviat scanned the forest. "Lower!" he shouted to the pilot. The helicopter dipped. Kiviat saw movement beneath the trees. "There!" he pointed.

In the jungle, Baby saw the horrible metal beast dive toward her with a deafening roar. For an instant, the dinosaur hatchling froze, then cried out and ran. The helicopter followed her.

Gambwe questioned Kiviat suspiciously. "Is *that* your treasure?"

"Yes," said Kiviat. "The most valuable living thing in the world."

Gambwe sneered. "You said gold." Grabbing a tranquilizer rifle Gambwe opened the chopper's main door and aimed at Baby.

The helicopter buzzed even lower, right over Baby's head. Terrified by the blowing dust and engine noise, Baby raced through prickly bushes and scratchy vines. She ignored the pain. Her fear drove her on.

Kiviat shouted, "Try for the neck!" Gambwe fired. The dart hit the ground an inch from Baby's foot.

Anger boiling inside him, George glanced back at the guard. The soldier was distracted by the action. George tensed his muscles. Kiviat screamed at the pilot, "Lower! Give him a better shot!"

Below, Baby zigzagged through the brush, fleeing in blind terror. Her skin was torn. Her energy and spirits were fading.

Gambwe fired again! The dart whizzed by Baby's ear.

Suddenly, George stood up, slamming into the guard. Pushing the startled man's machine gun aside, George whirled and smashed his fist into the soldier's face. The guard reeled back and dropped his gun. George punched him again, and the guard's head hit the chopper's wall.

Gambwe whirled and charged. Dodging, George karate-chopped the sergeant in the neck, then pushed hard. Gambwe stumbled backward and tumbled out of the chopper's open door. Screaming, the sergeant fell to his death, crashing into a thorny tree a hundred feet below.

Susan scrambled for the guard's gun, but Kiviat tackled her. Seizing the weapon, the evil professor tried to point it at Susan, but George kicked him in the stomach.

A burst of shots fired wildly!

A stray bullet ripped into the pilot's arm. The helicopter spun out of control. Kiviat, George and Susan were flung about. Kiviat clutched the gun. Blood spewing from his wounded arm, the pilot fought to regain control.

Below, Baby watched the sputtering chopper spin crazily. The metal beast barely missed a bank of trees, then plunged toward the river.

Wrestling with the controls, the pilot straightened the helicopter ten feet above the water. Kiviat fired again, but missed as the chopper climbed abruptly. Concentrating, Kiviat aimed the weapon. George saw only one chance for escape. Ducking, he grabbed Susan, and together they leaped through the open door, plunging into the river.

Kiviat screamed at the wounded pilot, "Go back! Turn! Get them!"

Happy to be alive, George and Susan swam to shore. Baby peeked through the trees. When the tiny dinosaur saw them, she bounced joyously from her hiding place and waggled her tail, acting more like a puppy than a reptile. George hugged her. Tears welled in Susan's eyes. Like a concerned mother, she said, "Baby, look at you! You're filthy!"

Covered with mud, Baby waddled happily over and licked Susan's face.

Then the threesome heard the chopper returning. Like a predatory bird, the helicopter appeared in the sky, diving toward them. Bullets again sprayed the trees and ground!

"Come on!" shouted George, leading them into the jungle. They raced off, the helicopter flying after them.

Inside the chopper, Kiviat screamed at the soldier who was still dizzy from his encounter with George. The wounded pilot pleaded, "I must land!"

George, Susan and Baby searched in desperation for a hiding place. Suddenly, George fell screaming into a hole in the jungle floor. Susan and Baby heard his cries and stopped, looking around, mystified. "I'm down here," called George.

Susan found the hole and peered down. George was brushing himself off, eight feet below on a rocky floor. They could hear the helicopter landing nearby.

"Come on!" George said. "It's some kind of cave."

Susan pushed Baby down, then climbed in, pulling brush over the hole. Groping around in the dark, she felt for George. "I can't see..."

Anxious voices sounded above them. George shushed Susan, then led her and Baby through the darkness, deeper into the cave. As they fled, they could hear running water echoing ahead.

Above, on the ground, Kiviat and the soldier searched for our heroes. Suddenly, the soldier pointed to a trail of Baby's footprints which led straight to the hidden opening.

Below, George, Susan and Baby emerged from the dark passageway into a wider, brighter cavern. In it were glittering stalactites and stalagmites. Dusty shafts of light appeared from holes in the crystalline ceiling. A fast stream of water flowed along the descending rock floor. The threesome splashed through the tiny river as they ran. Baby, trying to keep up, often hydroplaned like a seal on her belly.

The water grew steadily deeper as they ran. Waterfalls flowing down the walls fed the expanding stream. Suddenly, the cavern diverged into two tunnels. George pulled Susan into one. Baby not concentrating, headed down the other. Realizing her mistake, she skidded around on her belly, holding her feet up.

Meanwhile, Kiviat and the gun-toting soldier rushed from the narrow passage through the cavern.

George heard their pursuers closing in. Spotting a row of enormous stalagmites, he whispered, "Behind here!" and the threesome hid behind the wet rock. Seconds later, Kiviat and the soldier ran past. George waited until their pursuers' footsteps sounded distant, then cautiously led Susan and Baby back the way they came.

Abruptly, the footsteps stopped. The soldier shouted, then fired his machine gun. Bullets slammed into rock by George's head.

All of a sudden, a swarm of squeaking bats filled the air, their filmy wings flapping wildly. Kiviat and the soldier swatted at the winged creatures. Susan screamed. A bat was tangled in her hair, trying to nip her skin with its sharp teeth.

Baby, seeing Susan's predicament, charged bravely forward. Catching the bat between her jaws, she bit it in half, then promptly spit it out.

Without further ado, the threesome ran back down the tunnel. Their pursuers, flailing through the bats, quickly gave chase.

George, Susan and Baby ducked into the other tunnel. The passageway twisted and turned, growing narrower, darker and deeper. They could hear Kiviat closing in. Seconds later, the tunnel widened into a grotto filled with an

underground pond of clear, turquoise water. George, Susan and Baby waded in. The little dinosaur honked with relief, preferring the water to the rock floor.

Moments later, Kiviat and the soldier appeared behind them. The soldier raised his machine gun to shoot, but Kiviat pushed the barrel down. "No! You'll hit the animal!"

George, Susan and Baby fled to the far end of the grotto. There the pool poured in a swift, roaring waterfall, plunging twenty feet down into a river churning with rapids. Trapped, George and Susan peered over the brink, and considered jumping.

Kiviat shouted, "Don't! The animal won't make it!"

George asked Baby, "You gonna take that?" Baby honked. Grabbing the little dinosaur by the neck and Susan by the hand, George screamed, "GERONIMO!" Together they leaped into the raging torrent.

Kiviat and the soldier waded quickly to the ledge and looked down. All they could see was rocks and whitewater. Kiviat tried to urge the soldier over the falls, barking, "Follow them!"

Shocked, the soldier backed up. "No way!" he screamed. "Are you crazy?"

The waterfall dumped George, Susan and a frightened Baby into the rapids below. Crashing through a narrow tunnel, they tried to slow down by grabbing the rock walls, but the current was too strong. Helplessly, they tumbled over another small waterfall.

The tunnel ceiling was now much lower. There was only a foot of air above the water, then just inches. George and Susan gasped for air, their faces scraping the rock overhead. Baby was sucked underwater. Then the river became an underground spring, and they were all forced down into it.

Certain they were going to die, each one faced painful thoughts of death. There seemed to be no escape.

And then, miraculously, George, Susan and Baby were flung out of a cliffside, down a waterfall and into a pond.

Exhausted and bruised, they surfaced, gulping air. Baby seemed to be barely conscious. George and Susan dragged her to shore.

They had landed in a jungle paradise. Beautiful flowers and colorful butterflies surrounded them. Lush green vegetation flourished under countless aquamarine waterfalls. Grateful to be alive, George and Susan embraced, then rushed to take care of Baby.

The dinosaur hatchling coughed feebly. Bruises and scratches covered her skin. Water dribbled from her open mouth.

George and Susan nursed the infant dinosaur. With washcloths formed from their clothes, they cleaned her wounds. Baby looked up at them hopelessly. She barely had enough strength to breathe.

Susan brushed flies away from the baby brontosaurus's face. Distraught, she said, "Oh, George, if she dies, all this craziness, me wanting to be famous... it's sick. I'm as bad as Kiviat."

George was relieved to hear her speak so honestly. Touching her face, he said, "No, you're wonderful. I'm crazy about you."

Susan fell into his arms.

That evening, Baby, ill and feverish, slept fitfully. Susan cradled the infant dinosaur, singing a lullaby. George gathered fruit, and they fed Baby by hand. Honking weakly, Baby nibbled at the food, then closed her eyes.

Concerned, George and Susan stayed awake most of the night, nursing the sick brontosaurus. By morning, however, they were sound asleep. Grunting, Baby suddenly woke up, yawned, and looked around. Seeing George and Susan, she struggled to her feet and honked. Then she tested her tail, swinging it back and forth. She was still weak, but better. Happily, she waddled over to the sleeping couple, nudged them, and honked loudly in George's ear.

Bleary-eyed, George and Susan woke up. And instantly, they hugged the little dinosaur.

The ordeal was over!

Soon Baby was eager to travel. Like a family reunited, George , Susan and Baby continued their journey. Making good progress, they reached the Sengha River by late afternoon. Approaching the bank, however, they stopped in their tracks.

Kiviat's expedition was on the water, a couple of hundred yards upstream. Baby's Mom, still tied to the raft, was being poled toward them. Instinctively, George and Susan ducked behind the trees. Baby, however, seeing her Mom,

bellowed loudly. Susan pulled Baby back, warning, "Shhhh! Bad men."

On the raft, Mama dinosaur heard her child's cry. Despite being drugged and dazed, she lifted her head and howled.

Baby went into a frenzy. Honking for joy, she bolted and plunged into the river. Immediately, George and Susan waded in and grabbed Baby's tail, but she wiggled free, swimming swiftly toward the raft. Susan started after Baby , but George pulled her back. "They'll see us." Sadly, they decided to hide again in the trees.

A soldier spotted Baby and yelled to Kiviat, who was in a rubber motorboat. Elated, Kiviat shouted a command, and the boat sped up to Baby. Kiviat tossed a rope over the tiny brontosaurus and roughly pulled her away from her mother toward shore.

Baby screamed. Her mother cried helplessly.

Hidden in the brush, George and Susan watched, powerless and overwhelmed with grief. Desolately, Susan moaned, "Well, she's alive. That's all I should want."

"No!" spat George angrily. His eyes narrowed to furious slits as he watched Kiviat drag Baby onto the opposite bank.

Gloating over the trembling dinosaur hatchling, Kiviat and Nigel imprisoned Baby in a bamboo cage. Her dinosaur Mom watched with a heavy heart. So did her human Mom and Dad, hidden nearby in the bush.

That night George and Susan grieved, sitting by a smoky campfire. Susan said sadly, "I was starting to believe we were her parents." Weeping, she turned to grab a log, then yelped, shocked. Standing silently behind them was Cephu and his Kaleri warriors.

George said, "You've got a way of dropping in on people."

Cephu led George and Susan to the river. His warriors were dragging Kenge's seaplane onto shore. Kenge, standing majestically on one of the plane's floats, greeted George and Susan.

It seemed Cephu had a plan.

Kiviat set up a riverside camp by a semi-modern village at the foot of a roadway leading to Ogbomosho. Barking orders, he directed the soldiers as they lifted Mama brontosaurus by winch onto a large truck.

Nearby, Nigel ran tests on Baby, who was in a bamboo cage in the back of a pickup. The little brontosaurus appeared dazed and lifeless, obviously drugged.

Suddenly, several soldiers shouted frantically, "Fire! FIRE!"

George was fanning a fire at the edge of the compound. As the flames spread, and the soldiers rushed to extinguish the blaze, George dashed along the riverbank.

George joined Susan, Cephu and twenty Kaleri warriors, hiding behind a stack of oil barrels. The Kaleri wielded bows, arrows and spears. Their faces were painted for battle.

Susan asked, "Where's Kenge?"

"We'll have to wait," said George.

A soldier rushing toward the fire saw sunlight reflecting off of a Kaleri warrior's spear. Instantly, the soldier shot the man.

Spears and arrows filled the air. Soldiers whirled, firing their rifles. George, Susan and the Kaleris were pinned down!

Then, as if on cue, Kenge's seaplane dove out of the sky. Within seconds, Kenge was heaving gasoline bombs onto the soldiers. Bright red flames burst throughout the compound. The soldiers panicked, trying to dodge the bombs.

George leaped up and shouted, "NOW!" With the Kaleri as cover, he and Susan raced toward the Mama brontosaurus. Cephu led a valiant charge behind them. The soldiers were losing!

Kiviat, sensing defeat, fled for the truck that held Baby. George saw him. Ducking spears and gunfire, George chased and tackled the wicked professor. They fought wildly. George was much stronger, but Kiviat grabbed a crowbar and hit George on the head. Dazed, George reeled, falling, and Kiviat jumped into the truck.

Frightened and confused, Baby honked weakly. Nigel ran toward the truck, shouting, "Eric! Wait for me!" but Kiviat ignored him. Starting the engine, Kiviat roared off.

George chased him on foot.

Meanwhile, Susan and the Kaleri chopped at the ropes binding Mom. As Kiviat's truck barreled past, Mama brontosaurus furiously lifted her head in time to see the evil professor kidnapping her infant.

Kiviat sped heedlessly through the battlefield, crashing through the compound gate just as Susan hacked through the last of Mom's ropes. Roaring "Har-*reeeewwww!*" Mama brontosaurus struggled to her feet and rushed after Kiviat. Smiling, Susan shouted, "Sic 'em!"

George, his head bloody, jumped on a military motorcycle. Susan ran toward him, and then together they raced after Mama and Kiviat.

Accelerator to the floor, Kiviat sped into the village, scattering natives. Mama dinosaur stormed after him, towering over the thatched huts. Terrified,

the villagers fled in all directions, screaming, "MOKELE MBEMBE! *MOKELE MBEMBE!*" The jungle monster was attacking, just as their legends had predicted!

Mama brontosaurus trumpeted deafeningly and smashed her foot down on a hut. Pounding forward, she swept her tail against the primitive docks. The village's fishing fleet exploded like toothpicks. Enraged, Mama crashed through a warehouse, dragging the walls with her. Natives dashed out of the way as she flung the broken structure off with one shake of her massive body.

Nigel raced into the village, chasing Mom with a tranquilizer gun. Seeing her, he stopped and aimed. As Mama rampaged on, she collided into an overhead power wire. The live wire snapped, sparks crackling. Whipping

wildly, the electrical wire fell upon Nigel. The professor's assistant dropped to the ground, a dead, smoldering heap.

Mom turned, confused. Gun-toting soldiers rushed into the village. Her tail swept toward them. The army men were eliminated before they could fire a shot.

Meanwhile, Kiviat drove recklessly on. Suddenly, a burning water tower collapsed in front of him. Tires screeching, Kiviat swerved and smashed into a hut. Gritting his teeth, Kiviat slammed the truck into reverse, gunned through the debris, and headed for the dusty main road. Bouncing around in the truck bed, Baby honked loudly, confused and terrified.

Mama dinosaur saw Baby and heard her cries. Blindly, she barreled through a cluster of fuel storage tanks. Moments later, just behind the enraged brontosaurus, the chemical soup exploded sky-high.

Reaching the main road, Kiviat smiled evilly. His victorious thoughts quickly vanished, however, when he glanced in his rearview mirror. Mama brontosaurus, thirty furious tons of galloping muscle, was right behind him!

Baby honked desperately as her mother closed in.

Suddenly, Mom caught up with the truck! Reaching down with her neck, she banged her chin against the windshield. Kiviat screamed. Running above and over the pickup, Mama brontosaurus kicked the vehicle back and forth between her legs.

Kiviat yanked the steering wheel, swerving wildly. Crashing through a burning shack, and skidding onto a side street at the village outskirts, he momentarily lost Mama brontosaurus.

Baby honked, and Kiviat looked out behind. George and Susan, riding through the smoke on the military motorcyle, were racing after him!

Intent, Kiviat still careened through the twisting streets. Eyes wide, Baby honked at George and Susan. Dust swirled around the speeding vehicles. George gunned the motorcycle alongside Kiviat's truck. Obsessed, the evil professor gripped the wheel, trying to turn away as Susan smashed the truck's side window with the same crowbar Kiviat had used on George.

Suddenly, the road narrowed and curved sharply. The truck spun out of control. George guided the cycle expertly as Kiviat's truck hit a ditch and rolled. Baby's cage was thrown clear of the wreck.

Bleeding, Kiviat crawled out of the smashed pickup. Looking frantically around, he saw the splintered cage. He moaned, then whirled. Towering above him, Mama dinosaur growled and *attacked*! Kiviat stumbled backward, his face white with terror. Bending, Mama brontosaurus snatched the evil professor in her jaws. Proudly, she raised her neck, head towering above the trees. Kiviat struggled and screamed.

George and Susan watched in shock. As Kiviat died, Susan buried her head on George's shoulder.

Then Susan saw Baby lying motionless in the broken cage. "*Baby*!" she cried. They ran to the dinosaur hatchling. In tears, Susan stroked Baby's brow. She bent to kiss her dear dinosaur child—and one of Baby's eyes popped open! the infant brontosaurus honked!

George and Susan were joyous. They hugged Baby, laughing and crying happily. Their celebration was cut short, however, as Mom crept up behind, growling. She thought George and Susan were hurting Baby.

Quickly, Baby honked, telling Mama that George and Susan were friends. Then Baby rushed to her real mother, and George and Susan watched, overwhelmed with emotion. Finally reunited, the two loving dinosaurs nuzzled each other affectionately.

Happy tears poured from George and Susan's eyes.

The battle over, Cephu and his victorious Kaleri warriors joined them silently. Smoke curled from the burning village behind them. Soon, Mama and Baby turned their backs on the human crowd and lumbered slowly toward the river. George and Susan followed, stopping at the bank.

The dinosaurs waded into the water. Pausing, Baby turned and gazed at George and Susan, her "human parents." They had shared adventure together, and the tiny dinosaur loved them dearly. Wistfully, Baby honked goodbye.

Mom, her strength and dignity restored, tenderly lowered her head and licked Baby, beckoning her to follow. Wading farther into the stream, Mama brontosaurus swam off. Turning, Baby followed.

George and Susan watched the dinosaurs. Amazed, Cephu and the Kaleri gathered around them. George hugged Susan and said, "They're going home...where they belong."

Susan wiped away tears and said, "But so many people saw them."

George smiled knowingly. "Do you know how many people have seen the Loch Ness Monster, the Abominable Snowman and Bigfoot?"

Susan considered it. "Another legend?"

"It will become one if we let it," said George.

Susan held him tightly. Paddling next to Mom, Baby turned one last time, and honked. Susan smiled and mused, "It was nice having a kid for a while. Maybe we ought to have one of our own."

Grinning, George held her close.

Swimming off in the emerald river, the dinosaurs disappeared, returning to their distant homeland, far from civilization. There they remain, hidden in their jungle paradise. As the years pass, many fantastic stories will be told about their existence, stories that will change with time...into *legends.*